DATE DUE			

ELEPHANTS

Written and edited by **Barbara Taylor Cork**

Consultant Miranda Stevenson BA PhD
Curator of Animals, Royal Zoological Society of Scotland

PUFFIN BOOKS

PUFFIN BOOKS
Published by the Penguin Group
Viking Penguin Inc., 40 West 23rd Street, New York, New York 10010, U.S.A.

First published in the USA in 1989 by Viking Penguin Inc.

First published in the UK in 1989 by Two-Can Publishing Ltd

1 3 5 7 9 10 8 6 4 2

Photograph Credits:
p.4 Bruce Coleman/Carol Hughes p.5 Ardea/Alan Weaving p.6 (top) Ardea/Clem Haagner (bottom) Barbara Taylor Cork p.7 (top) Bruce Coleman/Dieter and Mary Plage (bottom) Bruce Coleman/Dieter and Mary Plage p.8/9 Bruce Coleman/Jen and Des Bartlett p.8 Bruce Coleman/Jen and Des Bartlett p.9 Bruce Coleman/Norman Myers p.10 (top) Bruce Coleman/R.I.M. Campbell (bottom) Ardea/Pat Morris p.11 NHPA/S. Robinson p.12 NHPA/Anthony Bannister p.13 Ardea/Clem Haagner p.12/13 Bruce Coleman/Jen and Des Bartlett p.14 NHPA/Steve Robinson p.15 Bruce Coleman/Jen and Des Bartlett p.16 (top) NHPA/John Shaw p.16 (bottom) Bruce Coleman/Simon Trevor p.17 (top) NHPA/Anthony Bannister (bottom) Ardea/Yann Arthus-Bertrand
Cover photo: Bruce Coleman/N. Myers

Illustration Credits:
p.1 Malcolm Livingstone p.3 Malcolm Livingstone/Alan Rogers p.4 Malcolm Livingstone p.9 Malcolm Livingstone p.11 Malcolm Livingstone p.14 Malcolm Livingstone p.18-19 Alastair Graham p.20-24 Malcolm Livingstone p.25 Alan Rogers p.27 Claire Legemah p.28-29 Malcolm Livingstone p.30 Tony Wells p.31 Alan Rogers p.32 Malcolm Livingstone

CONTENTS

LOOKING AT ELEPHANTS

Elephants are very strong, intelligent animals which live in the grasslands and forests of Africa and Asia. There are two kinds of elephant – the African and the Indian (or Asian) elephant. Elephants are the biggest animals that live on land. Male elephants are bigger than female elephants. They are called bulls and female elephants are called cows.

The elephant has a very good sense of smell and sharp hearing but its eyes are small and it can't see far ahead. To help it keep cool, the elephant waves its big ears back and forth.

African elephants and male Indian elephants have two long teeth called tusks, which grow out from the sides of the mouth. The tusks are made of ivory – the name elephant comes from the Hebrew word *elaph,* which means ivory.

▶ Right. The elephant's trunk is a very long nose and top lip joined together. It uses the trunk as a hand and a nose.

▶ Far right. The elephant strides along quite fast on its flat, cushionlike feet. It can't trot, jump or gallop because it is so heavy.

ELEPHANT FACTS

A big African elephant bull weighs about 6 tonnes (13,440 pounds) — as much as 90 people or 6 cars.

An elephant's tusks are sharp enough to go through the metal of a car.

AFRICAN ELEPHANTS

The pictures on these two pages will help you tell the difference between an African and an Indian elephant.

Dip in back   Big ears

Rounded forehead

Long tusks

Trunk with ridges

The African elephant is bigger than the Indian elephant.

Two fingers at tip of trunk

ELEPHANTS AT WORK

For thousands of years people have captured wild elephants and trained them to carry heavy loads, to take part in ceremonies and even to carry soldiers into battle. Nowadays, most working elephants are born in captivity.

INDIAN ELEPHANTS

Is the elephant on page 5 an African or an Indian elephant?

Small ears

Back arches upwards

Forehead sticks out

Short tusks (or no tusks)

Smooth trunk

One finger at tip of trunk

◀ Left. These elephants are taking part in a religious procession in Sri Lanka. They are wearing special cloths which are decorated with beautiful patterns.

◀ Far left. In this elephant training camp, the elephants are being taught to lift and pull heavy logs. The trainer taps or nudges the elephant with his feet or knees to tell it what to do.

ELEPHANT FAMILIES

In the wild, elephants like to live with other elephants in family groups of about eight members. The elephants in each group get on well together and help to look after each other, especially if one becomes sick or is injured. The young elephants need special protection because they could be attacked by enemies such as lions or hyenas.

Each family group consists of female elephants that are related to each other. In the group, there are mothers, aunts, cousins and their young ones. The strongest female usually leads the group; she is often the oldest elephant.

Female elephants stay with their family group for life (unless the group gets too big) but males leave the group when they are 12 to 16 years old. Then they live in all-male groups or on their own. From time to time, adult bulls may join a female family group.

▶ At a water hole, the oldest elephants drink or bathe first. Calves may have to wait more than an hour to get a drink.

▼ Several family groups sometimes stay together for a time to form a larger group of up to 50 or even 100 elephants. This is called a herd. Can you think of the names for some other large groups of animals?

An elephant often puts the end of its trunk into another elephant's mouth to say "Hello."

◀ Elephants often pretend to charge at enemies to drive them away. They hold their ears out to the side to make themselves look bigger and make a lot of snorting and trumpeting noises. A real charge often starts without warning. The elephant holds its trunk to one side and pushes its sharp tusks forward.

THE SEARCH FOR FOOD

Elephants are so big they need to eat a huge amount of food. They spend as much as 16 hours a day searching for food. They eat about 170 kilograms (375 pounds) of food every day.

Elephants are vegetarians. They eat all sorts of plant material from leaves and grasses to fruits, roots and tree bark. Can you find out what zoo elephants are given to eat.

The elephant may use its sharp tusks to help with feeding. The tusks grow all through the elephant's life but they don't get too long because they wear down as the elephant uses them. An elephant uses one tusk more than the other, in the same way that people are right- or left-handed.

▲ With its long trunk, the elephant can reach leaves high in the trees.

▼ This elephant is using its tusks to tear off strips of tasty tree bark.

To help them grind up tough plants, elephants have huge teeth with sharp ridges along the tops. An elephant has only about four teeth in its mouth at any one time. As each tooth wears away, a new tooth grows to take its place. An elephant grows 24 teeth during its life. When the last four teeth have worn away, the elephant can't chew its food, so it will die.

As elephants feed, they produce huge mounds of dung, which helps to make the soil rich.

▶ Elephants may cause a lot of damage to the countryside. They flatten the grasses and bushes and kill the trees by stripping off the bark.

FOOD FACTS

One tooth from an adult elephant weighs about 4.5 kilograms (10 pounds).

Elephants are so strong, they can push over trees to reach the tasty new leaves on the top branches.

Elephants like to eat salt; it helps them stay healthy. They may dig up salt with their tusks.

In 24 hours, ten elephants can make one ton (2,240 pounds) of dung.

MUD AND DUST BATHS

Every day, elephants plaster a thick
layer of mud over their skin. The
mud helps stop the skin from
getting dry and cracked and
protects it from insect bites. The
mud also helps to heal cuts.

In the photograph above, can you see the dust shooting out of one elephant's trunk? Elephants often squirt dust over themselves. The dust works like the mud to help protect their skin.

BABY ELEPHANTS

A female elephant is old enough to have her first baby when she is about 12 to 15 years old. She usually has one baby at a time. Baby elephants are called calves. The mother carries her calf inside her body for almost two years; no other animal is pregnant for such a long time.

When it is time for a mother to have her calf, she sometimes leaves the family group. Another female, called an auntie, stays near the mother. The mother elephant gives birth standing up. The newborn calf is quite hairy and has milk teeth called tushes. Only a few hours after it is born, the calf can walk but it is still very wobbly on its legs. When the calf is about two days old, it can move well enough to keep up with the rest of the group.

▲ The calf drinks its mother's rich milk from two teats which are between her front legs. The calf sucks milk with its mouth, not with its trunk. As it sucks, it holds its trunk out of the way.

▶ For the first few months of its life, the calf stays close to its mother but the other elephants in the group help to look after the tiny youngster.

One cow elephant can have as many as 4 calves in her life.

CALF FACTS

A newborn calf is about 1 meter (3 feet) tall and weighs about 120 kilograms (265 pounds) — as much as two people.

The calf takes about 6 months to learn how to use its trunk.

GROWING UP

When the baby elephant is a few months old, it starts to wander a little further from its mother and explore its surroundings. The mother still keeps a close watch on her calf's movements and is always ready to help if it is in trouble.

There is a lot for the young elephant to learn. It has to find out how to suck up water with its trunk and which sort of plants are good to eat. Although it drinks its mother's milk for at least two years, the calf starts to eat grass and other plants when it is about six months old. The calf may take some food from its mother's mouth to see what it tastes like.

The calf also has to learn the rules and customs of the group and sort out its own place within the family.

▲ The calf stays with its mother until it is 12-14 years old; mother elephants look after their young longer than any animal except humans.

▼ The young calf is very playful. It chases leaves or birds, pretends to charge and climbs over resting elephants. Playing helps the calf to learn how to take care of itself.

SAVE THE ELEPHANT

Today, both African and Indian elephants are struggling to survive. There are about 750,000 African elephants and 30,000 Indian elephants left in the wild. The main problem facing elephants is lack of space. Elephants need vast areas of land to find enough food and much of the land they used to live on is now full of villages and crops.

Most African elephants now live in National Parks. People are not usually allowed to kill elephants in a National Park. But the elephants may still be killed by poachers because their ivory tusks are worth a lot of money. Inside the National Parks, the elephants don't have enough room to spread out if their numbers increase. So, from time to time, some elephants may have to be killed to leave enough room for the rest of the elephants to survive. Elephants may also be shot if they damage crops or houses.

Elephants are not in danger of dying out today, but they may become extinct in the future if we don't look after them now.

◄ Elephants are often killed for their valuable tusks.

▼ Adult elephants, are so big and strong they have no real enemies apart from people. We must leave enough space for elephants to live in peace.

NTOTO'S BIG ADVENTURE

BY JANIS NOSTBAKKEN

The high midday sun was burning bright, beating down on the African plain where Ntoto, the baby elephant and the rest of his elephant family lived.

For the moment, the elephants had found shelter from the heat in a grove of trees. Here there was food to eat. The older elephants stretched their long trunks up to the very tops of the trees, while the younger ones made do with what they could find on the lower branches. Ntoto, the smallest of them all, was happy to stay close to Tembo, his mother, and eat the food she gathered for him.

Every now and then, Tembo would wrap her trunk around some tender leaves and pass them to Ntoto.

Sometimes, when Ntoto thought he'd waited too long between mouthfuls, he would use his trunk to reach right into Tembo's mouth and take the food she was eating. Tembo didn't mind. She knew that it wouldn't be long before her calf was fending for himself. In the meantime, she kept a watchful eye over him, teaching him all she could about life on the plains.

Ntoto played in the shade of his mother's shadow, moving in and out between her legs and sometimes resting right under her huge body. From time to time, he'd reach up and nuzzle her or tug at her tail with his trunk, but Tembo was too busy eating to stop and play.

So Ntoto decided to join his

cousins. Some of them were having a game of tug-of-war. They coiled their long noses around each other's and pulled and pulled. Ntoto wanted to play, too. He touched his trunk to theirs to say hello and the youngsters stopped to greet their cousin. Before long, all the young calves were hugging and tugging and pushing and pulling each other. Their game ended in a chase and Ntoto was soon scrambling back to Tembo's side.

By this time, the older elephants had stripped the trees bare and had begun feeding on the sweet grass that grew nearby. Ntoto watched Tembo as she wrapped her trunk around a clump of grass and pulled it out. She beat the grass against her leg to shake off any loose dirt before lifting it up to her mouth.

Ntoto copied Tembo's every move. He grabbed a tuft of grass with his trunk and pulled it out of the ground.

It worked! Then he shook off the loose soil and put the grass into his mouth.

The sun was directly overhead and the heat was almost unbearable. Ntoto's aunt, the oldest and biggest elephant of the family, signaled to the others that it was time to move on. The elephants followed after her on their way to the waterhole.

Ntoto meant to leave with the rest of the herd, but in his haste he tripped over his own trunk and fell flat on the ground! Tembo came to his rescue. She wound her trunk around him, picked him up and set him on his four feet once more. Then they hurried to catch up with the other elephants.

As they moved across, the savanna, Ntoto saw many other animals. He spotted a herd of zebra, and behind them, some gazelle gracefully gliding by. He just had to stop and watch. But the rest of the

elephants marched on and Tembo finally had to pull Ntoto along by the trunk to make sure he kept up with the others.

Eventually the elephants arrived at the waterhole. Ntoto wanted to plunge right in. But that wouldn't do. The leader of the group always took her turn first, followed by the other grown-ups. The calves would have to wait.

Ntoto stood at the top of the steep slope that led to the water's edge and watched his aunts slip and slide down the river bank. He wasn't so sure he wanted to go now that he saw how hard it was. The little elephant hung back but when his turn came, Tembo coaxed him to the edge and before he knew it, he was tumbling down the side, landing with a smack right in the muddy river bed! Ntoto was delighted. Over and over he rolled, covering himself in

the slimy mud which soothed his hot, dry skin.

The others had already waded into the water until they were almost completely submerged. Only the tops of their heads and the tips of their trunks were showing.

Ntoto was thirsty. He stepped through the sticky mud and took a drink. First, he sucked in the water through his trunk and then tried to spray it into his mouth. But Ntoto's aim wasn't quite on target. The water splashed all over his face! Never mind. He'd have a shower as well as a bath. His cousins joined in the fun, spraying and splashing and playing water tag.

Tembo came to tell them it was time to end their game and move on. The other elephants had already begun to climb up the river bank and it would be no easy task for the little ones.

The elephants gained as much speed as they could and hurled themselves up the slope. One by one, they made their way to the top and heaved their big bodies over the edge of the river bank.

Ntoto wasn't sure he could make it. Tembo went ahead to show him how, and he tried his best. But when he got near the top, he slid back down again. Once, twice, three times he scrambled up the slope, the third time landing upside down in the mud. Tembo patiently waited and urged him to try once more. Ntoto struggled to his feet and made another rush up the slope. Higher and higher he climbed. He was almost there! Tembo dangled her powerful trunk in front of him. Could he reach it? He stretched out his own trunk and just managed to grab hold of his mother's. She pulled with all

her might until, at last, Ntoto was safe at the top.

Once everyone was together again, the herd headed for a dust pit for their after-the-bath powdering. They sucked up dirt and dusted themselves all over. Ntoto loved showering himself with sand, and besides, it helped protect his skin from itchy bug bites.

The elephants ambled on under the cloudless sky until they came to another grove of trees. Some of them began to feed on the leaves. Others had a good scratch by rubbing themselves against the tree trunks. But Tembo just rested. She stood in the shade, fanning herself with her broad ears, flapping them back and forth. Ntoto did the same, but not for long. He wanted to explore. So while Tembo dozed, Ntoto followed his nose across the grassy fields.

Suddenly, a loud trumpeting rang out through the air! Danger was near. The lead elephants sounded the alarm as the other adults formed a circle around their young ones.

But where was Ntoto? Tembo couldn't find him anywhere. What if a hungry hyena or lion was lurking nearby? A little elephant would be just the meal for him.

Off in the distance, Ntoto had heard the elephant's warning call. As fast as he could, he raced back to his family. What could be wrong? His mother saw him hurrying along and rushed him into the inner circle with his cousins.

Ntoto was frightened. He watched the lead elephant defend the herd. She stood tall, trumpeting wildly, stomping her huge feet to ward off any intruder. Not many animals would be willing to battle with such a fierce warrior.

The elephants waited and waited until, at last, they were certain the danger had passed. Ntoto hurried to Tembo's side and stayed close.

That day, Ntoto had learned an important lesson. Never again would he wander far from the herd. He knew his place was with his mother.

And so, side by side, Ntoto and Tembo and the rest of the family continued on their way across the African plain.

SPOT THE DIFFERENCE

Can you spot ten differences between these two pictures?

ELEPHANT MASK

There are lots of ways to decorate masks. Here are a few things to try.

yarn

string

straws

crayons

brown

white

red

paint

fabric

colored paper

► This mask was made by drawing the basic shape on to cardboard and decorating it with colored paper.

Making a mask is easy. All you have to do is draw a mask shape on to a piece of cardboard or thick paper. Remember to make two holes for your eyes and a small hole at each side of the mask. Carefully cut out your mask and then decorate it. Finally, thread a piece of elastic, string or lace through the small holes at the sides of the mask.

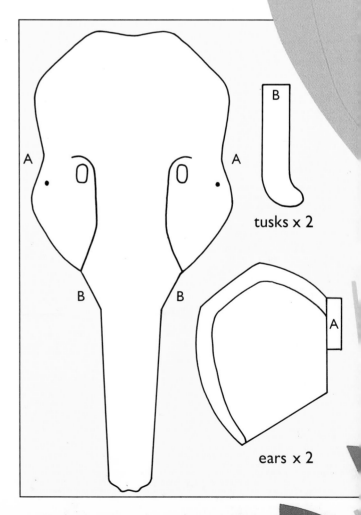

A

A

B

B

B

tusks x 2

A

ears x 2

FIND THE ELEPHANTS

There are six elephants hiding in this picture? Can you find them all?

There is one more animal in the picture. Do you know its name?

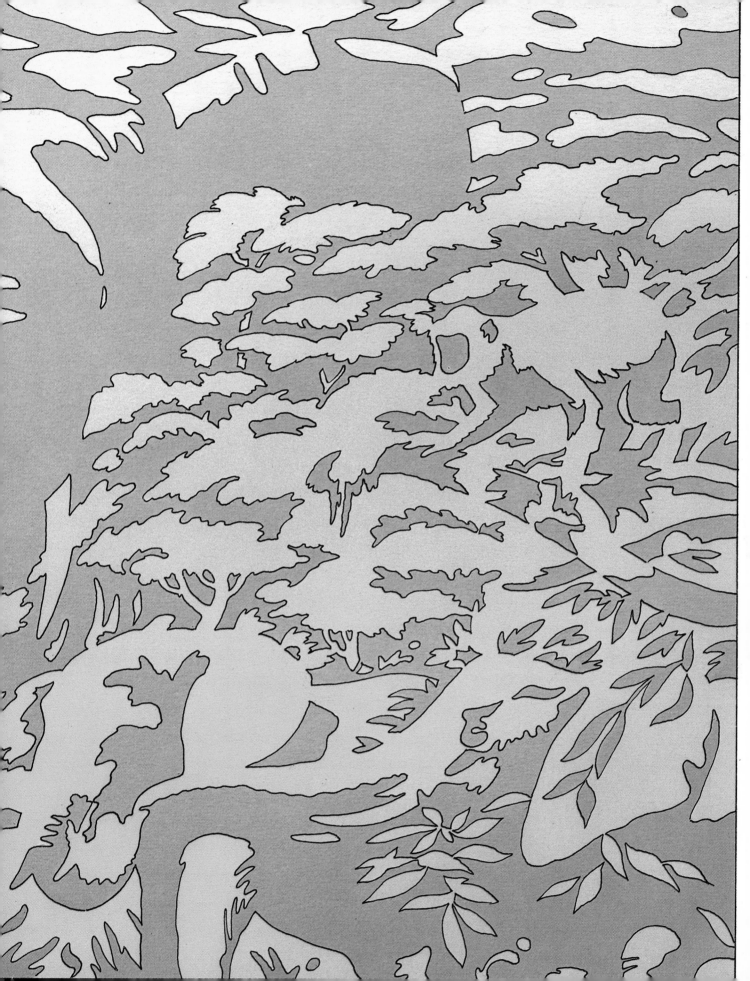

FOOT PRINT MAZE

Can you help this baby elephant find its mother?

TRUE OR FALSE?

Which of these facts are true and which ones are false? If you have read this book carefully, you will know the answers.

1. Elephants are the biggest animals that live on land.
2. Elephants flap their ears back and forth to keep cool.
3. An elephant's trunk is a nose and top lip joined together.
4. African elephants don't have tusks.

5. The African elephant is bigger than the Indian elephant.
6. Indian elephants have bigger ears than African elephants.
7. Elephants like to eat tree bark.

8. An elephant has lots of very small teeth.
9. An elephant's tusks stop growing when it is 12 years old.

10. An elephant is so strong, it can push a car along.
11. An elephant likes to plaster itself with mud and dust.

12. A baby elephant sucks its mother's milk with its trunk.
13. A mother elephant looks after her calf for 2 years.
14. An elephant can gallop as fast as a horse.

ANSWERS: 1. True; 2. True; 3. True; 4. False; 5. True; 6. False; 7. True; 8. False; 9. False; 10. True; 11. True; 12. False; 13. False; 14. False.

INDEX